CHILI POWDER

GREEN PEPPERS

CARROTS

GARLIC

ONIONS

TOMATOES

BEANS

Dear Pig Fans,

Pigs In The Pantry: Fun With Math and Cooking is the third title in the Pigs Will Be Pigs math series. It's all about MEASUREMENT of LIQUID and SOLID QUANTITIES! When I was in elementary school, that word frightened me, as did just about everything that had to do with math. I never realized that math was all around us in our daily lives. That's why I wrote the Pigs Will Be Pigs books, which (by the way) are all based on true family adventures. My husband loves to cook, but, he doesn't always pay attention to the recipe. One time, after he made spaghetti that no one would eat, I had a great idea—putting Mr. Pig in charge of the kitchen would be a way to learn about measurement of liquid and solid quantities. So follow these easy steps:

1) Read **Pigs In The Pantry** just for fun!

2) Go back and read the story again. Pay close attention to the recipe. Figure out where Mr. Pig and the piglets went wrong and how much of each ingredient they should have used.

3) Make Firehouse Chili with your family. Be a good cook and measure acurately. Have all of your ingredients and measuring cups and spoons handy.

4) Answer the math questions at the end of the book. You can do this by yourself, with your parents, or with your teacher.

Remember the Pig Family Motto:

MATH + READING = FUN

Love,

Amy Axelrod

P.S. For Parents and Teachers Only
The Pigs Will Be Pigs books have been designed around the National Council of Teachers of Mathematics's Thirteen Standards. Use them as picture book read-alouds initially, and then as vehicles to introduce, reinforce, and review the concepts and skills particular to each title.

Pigs in the Pantry

Fun with Math and Cooking

story by **Amy Axelrod**

pictures by **Sharon McGinley-Nally**

Aladdin Paperbacks

Mrs. Pig was under the weather.

"I'm all stuffed up," she sniffled. "And I ache all over."

"Dear, you stay put," insisted Mr. Pig. "What you need is rest."

"Let's make Mom her favorite dish," suggested the piglets. "That'll pick her right up."

"Great idea," said Mr. Pig, "except for one thing."

"What's that?" asked the piglets.

"I don't know my way around the kitchen very well," he said. "Do you?"

The piglets shook their heads no.

"No problem," said Mr. Pig. "How difficult can it be?"

"You're absolutely right, Dad," said the piglets. "There's nothing we can't handle."

"Well, then," said Mr. Pig, "there's only one thing to do . . ."

LET'S

Mr. Pig and the piglets washed up and put on aprons.
"Your mother doesn't know it yet," said Mr. Pig, "but today
is her lucky day. Now, where does she keep the pots and pans?"
"We don't know," said the piglets. "We'll go ask her."

Mr. Pig reached up above the stove and took down
Mrs. Pig's favorite cookbook from the center shelf.
"Herc we go," he said.
Mr. Pig studied the recipe.

Please ask an adult for help!

Firehouse Chili

(made with fresh vegetables)

Serves 4 hearty eaters.

Ingredients

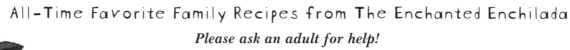

Vegetables

6 cups of the following:

- pinto beans or
- black beans or
- red kidney beans or
- pink beans or
- small white beans

Use any one type of bean or combine as many different types as you like.

- 1/4 cup olive oil + 2 tablespoons *(for frying)*
- 4 large white onions, chopped *(or 2 huge white onions)*

- garlic cloves, minced (at least 2, but not more than 6)
- 5 or 6 carrots, diced
- 3 green peppers, sliced
- 3 red peppers, cubed
- 1 dozen large, ripe, juicy tomatoes, chopped or crushed
- 1 to 1 1/2 cups tomato juice or water
- * *optional:* for variety, add sliced mushrooms, celery, and/or zucchini

Spices

- coarse salt, a dash or two
- freshly ground pepper, to taste
- cayenne pepper, a pinch
- 1 teaspoon paprika
- 1 teaspoon cumin
- 1 teaspoon dried basil

- chili powder *(use heaping spoonfuls)*
  - ★ 1 tablespoon: 1 ALARM, a hint of spice
  - ★ 2 tablespoons: 2 ALARM, definitely spicy
  - ★ 3 tablespoons: 3 ALARM, hot, hot, hot
  - ★ 4 tablespoons: 4 ALARM, hair-raising
  - ★ 5 tablespoons: 5 ALARM, call the firehouse
  to put out the fire!
  ★*For those who live dangerously:* add 2 chopped jalapeño peppers

Directions

Step 1 Drain beans and rinse thoroughly. Very important! Measure by packing tightly in measuring cup and set aside in bowl.

Step 2 Sauté chopped onions, minced garlic, diced carrots, and sliced and cubed peppers in olive oil in a large frying pan until soft and slightly browned. Use a low flame. Stir frequently. Be careful never to burn.

Step 3 Transfer vegetables into a deep pot. Add beans, tomatoes, and juice or water. Combine thoroughly. Mix in spices. Stir. Cover pot with lid. First bring to a boil, then reduce heat and simmer uncovered for 30–45 minutes. Do not forget to stir frequently in order to prevent sticking.

Step 4 Add more tomato juice or water if chili is too thick.

Step 5 Serve hot with grated Monterey Jack cheese or sharp cheddar cheese on top and crispy nachos on the side.

Step 6 Enjoy!

"Mom says the pots and pans are on the shelf behind the popcorn maker inside of the cabinet between the sink and the dishwasher," said the piglets.

"Sure enough," said Mr. Pig, taking out some pots and pans, "but I forgot to have you ask her where she keeps the measuring spoons."

"We'll be right back," said the piglets.

"Mom says to look in the second drawer down," said the piglets.

"You didn't spill the beans, did you?" asked Mr. Pig.

"Oh, no," said the piglets. "All we did was tell Mom that today would be her lucky day."

"Good," said Mr. Pig.

Mr. Pig went to the pantry. "Hmmm, these are your mother's favorite color," he said, as he handed the piglets five large cans of pink beans. Mr. Pig also picked out an assortment of spices.

The Pigs placed everything on the counter between the stove and the sink. Mr. Pig opened all five of the cans and dumped the beans into a pot. Then he sent the piglets out to the garden for vegetables. "Nothing but the freshest for your mother," he reminded them.

While the piglets rooted around in the garden, Mr. Pig glanced at the recipe for a second time. Then he returned the cookbook to its place on the shelf.

Mr. Pig diced three onions, chopped eight cloves of garlic, cubed one carrot, minced five green peppers, and chopped seven red peppers, while the piglets watched. Then he placed all of the vegetables in a frying pan and poured in four cups of oil. "Not too low," he told the piglets, while he turned up the heat, "or they'll never cook."

"Don't forget about the tomatoes," said the piglets.

"My thoughts exactly," said Mr. Pig.

"Dad, don't you think the veggies are burning?" asked the piglets.

"Nonsense," said Mr. Pig. "They're a little well done, just the way your mother likes them."

Mr. Pig opened the back door and turned on the stove fan. Then he scraped the vegetables into the pot of beans and added the crushed tomatoes.

"Now for the spices," said Mr. Pig. "Let's see, the recipe calls for a dash of paprika, two-thirds of a cup of salt, and a cup and a half of pepper."

"Add lots of chili powder," said the piglets. "We need to clear Mom's stuffy nose."

Mr. Pig stirred ten tablespoons of chili powder into the mixture, turned the heat back on high, and covered the pot.

"Let's go have a snack and watch some TV while the chili cooks," said Mr. Pig.

"Do you hear that siren?" asked the piglets after a few minutes. Mr. Pig and the piglets ran back to the kitchen just as Mrs. Pig awoke from her nap.

"I feel refreshed," said Mrs. Pig. "That nap did me a world
of good. It's even stopped raining. My, look at that beautiful rainbow!"

Mrs. Pig put on her bathrobe and
went downstairs.

"I think the children are right," she said . . .

"today sure is my lucky . . ."

For M. W.
—A. A.

For Chef Leroux,
1996 Chili King of Alachua County, Florida, a
creator of the famous Buzzard's Bread
Three Meat Chili
—S. M-N.

WHAT DOES MR. PIG NEED TO LEARN ABOUT COOKING?

When you measure you figure out the amount of something. Measurement is a means of comparison. Measurement in cooking allows the chef to compare amounts and get the mix of ingredients right.

Measurement Facts

a pinch	=	the small amount you can pinch with your fingers
a dash	=	several quick dashes or drops (less than 1/8 of a teaspoon)
1 teaspoon	=	1/3 of a tablespoon
1 tablespoon	=	3 teaspoons
2 tablespoons	=	1/8 of a cup = 1 ounce
4 tablespoons	=	1/4 of a cup = 2 ounces
8 tablespoons	=	1/2 of a cup = 4 ounces
16 tablespoons	=	1 cup = 8 ounces
2 cups	=	1 pint = 16 ounces
2 pints	=	1 quart = 32 ounces
2 quarts	=	1/2 of a gallon = 64 ounces
2 half gallons	=	1 gallon = 128 ounces

Some words cooks use

Chop—to cut into pieces
Cube—to cut into cubes
Dice—to cut into small cubes
Mince—to cut or chop into very small pieces
Crush—to pound or grind into small particles
Sauté—to fry in a small amount of butter or oil
Simmer—to stew gently
Boil—to heat to the boiling point
Recipe—instructions for preparing something from various ingredients

Metric Facts

1 teaspoon = 5 milliliters

1 tablespoon = 15 milliliters

1 cup = 240 milliliters

(metric conversions are approximate)

Mr. Pig made many mistakes in the kitchen because he did not follow the recipe. What are three of those mistakes?
How many teaspoons are there in one cup?

Bonus question:
How many extra beans did Mr. Pig put into the chili?

CHILI POWDER

GREEN PEPPERS

CARROTS

ONIONS

GARLIC

TOMATOES

BEANS

½ ¼
¾
½ ¼ 3
¾
½ ¼ 2
¾
½ ¼ 1
¾
½ ¼

4